D0627114

To mark
from Grandma

Other **LADYBIRD** Titles:—

Sole distributors in the U.S.A.

CHRISTIAN LITERATURE CRUSADE
FORT WASHINGTON   PENNSYLVANIA 19034

The story of
PETER
the Fisherman

by D. S. HARE

with illustrations by
ERIC WINTER

Publishers: Wills & Hepworth Ltd., Loughborough
First published 1970 © *Printed in England*

PETER THE FISHERMAN

Many years ago, a man called Simon lived in a cottage by the Sea of Galilee. He was a big man, tall and strong, and a fisherman. With his brother Andrew, he sailed his fishing-boat, and the fish they caught were sold in the markets nearby.

After Simon had married, he moved to a bigger house where Andrew could stay and where his wife's mother could live as well. This was at Capernaum, a town of some size on the shore of the Sea of Galilee.

They worked with James and John, the sons of old Zebedee, and spent their days fishing, mending their nets, and keeping their boats in trim. Sometimes they fished at night.

It was a strenuous life, not one for a weakling, and dangerous too, for sudden storms would sweep down from the surrounding hills and then the sea became very rough.

Simon and others fishing.

0 7214 0274 7

One day a strange figure, dressed in animal skins, appeared in the district nearby. He was a prophet, and he called on the people to repent, to ask God to forgive their wrongs and to help them to turn from wicked ways. Andrew was attracted by this man's preaching, and became one of his followers.

This prophet, John, lived mainly in the desert, but preached by the River Jordan and baptised in it.

Andrew told Simon about the prophet's teaching, how John preached continually that Someone far greater than he was coming soon, God's Chosen One. Then one day John pointed out his cousin Jesus to his followers and said, "There you are; there is God's Chosen One. Follow me no more, but follow Him."

Andrew ran to tell Simon. "We have found the Messiah!" he said, and took Simon to Jesus.

John the Baptist with Andrew.

When Jesus saw Simon, He looked steadily at him and said, "So you are Simon! I am going to call you Peter, because that means 'a rock'!" Simon was puzzled, but he was at once attracted by this man who spoke with such power.

Next day Simon and Andrew went to the place of worship, the synagogue, for Jesus was preaching there. Jesus taught so well that the people were astonished. After He had preached, He healed a man sick in mind, and this amazed everyone there.

Simon invited Jesus back to his house after the service. He found that his wife's mother was very ill with a high fever. When Jesus heard this He went to see her. He took her by the hand, and at once the fever left her. She felt so much better that she got up and helped to fetch the supper for their guests.

Jesus heals Simon's mother-in-law.

That evening all the sick people of the village came to Jesus, for they had heard about Him curing a man in the synagogue. Simon watched with wonder as Jesus healed every one of the sick people.

Eventually Jesus returned to the house, tired out. He spent the night at Simon's house, but in the morning His room was empty. Simon searched everywhere and went through the town but could not find Him.

Others were now looking for this wonderful healer and teacher. Then they saw Him up on the hillside alone. They scrambled up and found Him praying.

"We have been looking for You everywhere," they said. "You must not leave us."

"I must," said Jesus. "I must go and preach the good news of the Kingdom of God in other places as well."

Then He left Capernaum.

The people find Jesus alone on a hill-top.

Simon Peter now had much to think about! This man, so calm and yet so bold, with His amazing power of healing – who was He? Was He the promised Messiah, God's Chosen One?

One day Simon was cleaning his net. He and Andrew, together with James and John, had been fishing all night long, but they had not caught a single fish.

Suddenly they saw a crowd of people heading towards the sea-shore. They were all following Jesus, but there were so many that they were not all able to hear Him. Jesus told them to sit down on the sloping bank of the sea-shore. Then He went over to Simon's boat, and climbed into the bow.

"Push out a little from the shore!" He called to Simon. So He taught the people from the boat, and they all heard Him.

12   *Jesus preaches to the crowd from the bow of Simon's boat.*

"Thank you, Simon Peter," said Jesus as He climbed out of the boat. "Now go out and catch some fish!"

Simon sighed. "Master," he replied, "we have been fishing all night and we have caught nothing." Jesus smiled at him. "Go and try now," He said, and Simon did as Jesus told him.

Andrew and Simon pushed off into deep water and, expecting nothing, let down their nets. Soon these were sagging, for they had made a huge catch. They started to haul in the nets, but there were so many fish that the nets began to break. They called to James and John to come and help them, for the catch was so heavy.

Simon was amazed and a little frightened. When they reached the shore, Simon ran and knelt before Jesus saying, "Leave me, Lord, I am only a sinful man."

Jesus replied, "Do not be afraid, Simon. From now on you will go fishing for men who will follow Me."

Andrew and Simon make a huge catch.

So Peter, as we must now call him, left his fishing and became a full-time disciple. He followed Jesus on His preaching tours around Galilee. Soon, about seventy people were with Jesus, for in every town more followers joined them.

One day on a mountain side, Jesus called twelve of his followers to Him. He told them they were to be His chosen disciples. Peter was among them. He listened attentively as Jesus taught them about His Kingdom of Love, where people would respect others as much as themselves and seek God's way and God's will rather than their own.

This inspiring message was eagerly accepted by the Jewish country people. They had a hard life because they were ruled by a bad king, Herod, and also by the Romans, who had conquered Palestine and demanded extra taxes.

Jesus calls twelve apostles.

Once an important synagogue ruler, named Jairus, came running to Jesus. "Come quickly, please," he said, "my little daughter is dying. Come and heal her." Jesus praised the man's faith and, followed by a large crowd, went with him.

On the way, a servant came and said to Jairus, "Your daughter has died. Do not trouble the Master any more." Jesus heard the message. "Do not be afraid," He said, "just have faith."

At Jairus' house, Jesus called Peter, James and John into the room with the girl's parents. Peter wondered what Jesus could do, for she lay dead in her bed.

Peter watched Jesus take her hand and gently say, "Get up, my child." The girl stirred, got up and walked about. They were all amazed. Peter could hardly realise that Jesus had actually given new life to the girl.

"Now," Jesus reminded them, "she will need something to eat."

Jesus brings Jairus' daughter back to life.

One afternoon, a huge crowd of about five thousand people was listening to Jesus at a quiet place on the shore. When evening came, Peter wanted Jesus to send them away to buy their food. Jesus replied, "They need not go away; you give them something to eat." Peter thought He must be joking. "We have only five rolls and a couple of fish," he replied. "How can we feed these thousands?"

Then Jesus told him to make the people sit in groups. He prayed over the few rolls and the fish, and told the disciples to give them out. To their astonishment, the supply never ran short; they were able to feed everyone. In fact, there were enough pieces left over to fill a dozen baskets.

The people, filled and satisfied now, went home. And Jesus went off to the hills alone, to pray.

Jesus feeds the multitude.

Jesus had told the disciples to sail across the Sea of Galilee in their boat. So they climbed in and set sail across the water. They did not question Jesus, they just obeyed.

Night came, and the wind began to increase. The sea became rough and rowing was hard, for the wind was against them. By this time they were far from the shore, struggling in the dark against the sea and the wind.

Suddenly they saw the figure of a man near them on the water. "It is a ghost!" cried one, terrified.

"Do not be afraid," called Jesus. "It is I. Have courage!" Then they recognised Him. It really was Jesus, walking towards them on the water.

"Lord," said Peter, "can I come to You on the water?"

"Come along!" said Jesus. So Peter, looking straight at Jesus, began to walk across the water towards Him.

The disciples see Jesus walking on the water.

Suddenly Peter felt frightened. He took his eyes off Jesus, looked down at the waves and began to sink.

"Lord, save me!" he cried out. Jesus reached out His hand and caught him.

"You must not doubt, but have faith," He said. Jesus and Peter joined the others in the boat and soon they were at the shore. "Truly, You are the Son of God," they all said.

Peter was learning a great many things by being with Jesus, but the most important was to trust the Lord completely. Jesus had not only taught His disciples about the Kingdom of God, but had also shown that God cares for each and every one of His children.

By giving life to a dead girl, feeding hungry thousands, and now walking over the water, He had shown both the power and the love of God.

24   *Peter walks to Jesus on the water.*

Peter was regarded by the other disciples as their leader. He found himself keeping in order the crowds who flocked to hear Jesus and to be healed by Him.

One day a crowd of children clustered around Jesus. "Get back, you youngsters," ordered Peter. "Can't you see the Master's tired out, and doesn't want you clamouring around Him?" And he began to turn them away.

But Jesus restrained him, saying, "Let the children all come to Me; don't stop them." So they came around Him, held His hand, and sat on His lap.

"Children," He said to His disciples, "are so trusting. And I say to you that unless you receive the Kingdom of God with child-like trust, you shall never enter it."

Peter felt ashamed, and wished that he hadn't been so quick to speak; but he had learnt another lesson from the Master.

Jesus calls children to Him.

By this time Peter had been with Jesus for nearly three years, travelling all over northern Palestine, teaching, preaching and healing. Now Jesus set out for Jerusalem.

One evening He talked to His disciples about going away from them, and yet not entirely leaving them. Then He took a towel and a basin, and solemnly went around to each man and washed his feet. Peter was horrified – this was a slave's work, not for his Master to do. He did not want Jesus to wash his feet.

"Not me, Lord!" he cried.

But Jesus answered, "If I do not wash you, Peter, you cannot be one of Mine."

"Then wash me all over, Lord," said Peter hastily. But Jesus just washed his feet. He said He had given them all an example.

"It is no good talking about loving other people," He explained, "without showing it in loving service to others."

Jesus washes Peter's feet.

Jesus told His disciples that He would be betrayed, and then He would go to a place where they could not follow. Peter was indignant.

"Why cannot I follow you, Lord?" he said. "I would die for You!"

"Would you?" said Jesus. "I tell you that this night, before the cock crows twice for the dawn, you will disown Me three times."

As they talked and prayed in the Garden that dark evening, a group of men approached. Their leader was Judas, a disciple. He greeted Jesus with a kiss, and then the soldiers with him seized Jesus.

Peter immediately grabbed a sword, struck out at a man and cut off his ear, but Jesus gently rebuked him.

"Put away your sword, Peter," He said. "It is not needed." He healed the man's ear, then was led away.

Peter followed at a distance, until Jesus was taken inside.

The arrest of Jesus.

Peter felt cold, so he went over to the open fire in the courtyard to warm himself. A servant girl looked closely at him and said, "Were you not with the man from Galilee – with Jesus?"

"No," replied Peter, "I do not know Him." As he walked away, a cock crowed.

The maid-servant told the others, "I am sure he is one of them." "No! I am not!" shouted Peter.

The others said, "You must be; you are from Galilee, too!"

Peter replied angrily, "I tell you, I do not know this man!" Then a cock crowed a second time, reminding Peter of Jesus' words. He went away and wept bitterly.

As daylight came, there was urgent activity every-where. Peter was told that three criminals were to be crucified – nailed alive to a large cross of wood. Then he learned with horror that one of the three was to be his own Lord and Master – Jesus.

Peter's denial.

Peter watched the Roman soldiers assemble and march off with the prisoners, each prisoner carrying his own cross. What a terrible end, he thought, for his loving, kind Master – to die like a criminal.

On a hill outside the city wall, first the two criminals, then Jesus between them, were nailed to the huge crosses. Peter watched with a heavy heart for as long as he could, and then went back to the other disciples.

He found them all afraid, downcast, upset. Soon the women came back, together with John. They had been comforting Mary, Jesus' mother. They told Peter that Jesus was dead, and that although it was only mid-afternoon, it was as dark as night outside.

That evening the women took precious ointments to wash the body of Jesus. It had been taken down from the cross and placed in a special tomb in the hillside by a man called Joseph. Then the entrance was sealed with a huge rock. As the next day was the Sabbath, or Day of Rest, they remained indoors.

The Crucifixion.

At dawn on the day after the Sabbath, Peter was praying. Suddenly Mary Magdalene rushed in, very upset. "I have just been to the tomb," she said breathlessly. "The stone has been rolled away, and the body is not there!"

Peter immediately ran to the tomb. Inside, he saw only the linen cloth that had been wrapped around the body. He walked back puzzled, deep in thought, leaving Mary weeping at the tomb.

Soon after, Mary Magdalene hurried in. "I have seen the Lord!" she exclaimed to their startled ears. "He is alive – and I have talked with Him!" But they did not believe her.

That evening, the disciples met behind locked doors. Suddenly they realised that Jesus was with them; He was there, talking to them, explaining that He had over-come death, encouraging them to believe and trust in Him.

Peter grasped the feet and hands of Jesus. "It really is You, Lord!" he exclaimed.

The empty tomb.

Jesus told Peter to return to Galilee and wait for Him there.

One evening, by the lakeside, Peter suddenly announced: "I am going fishing." "We will join you," said the others. So they went out and fished all night, but caught nothing.

As dawn broke, a man on the shore called to them, "Have you caught anything?" When they said they had not, he replied, "Throw out your net on the other side!" They did so – and caught so many fish that they were unable to pull in the net. John said to Peter, "Surely it is the Lord!"

Peter jumped into the water and hurried to the shore. Jesus had a fire ready for cooking their breakfast. They were amazed and said little. Then Jesus turned to Peter.

"Do you really love me, Simon Peter?" He asked.

"Yes, Lord," replied Peter.

"Then," said Jesus, "feed My flock."

Peter's miraculous catch.

Jesus had meant that Peter was to look after the believers, the first Christians, and to give up his fishing. So they returned to Jerusalem, and a little while later they all met on a hill called the Mount of Olives, outside the city. There it was that Jesus came to them for the last time.

"Now I must return to My Father," He said, "but you will receive a Power within you, the Spirit of God, which My Father will send you. Then you must spread My teaching, not only here in Jerusalem, not only in Palestine, but throughout the whole world."

When He had said this He seemed to be taken up in front of their eyes until a cloud hid Him from their sight. Then two angels stood by them and assured them that although they would not see Jesus again, He would always be with them.

Full of hope and new courage, the disciples went back to the city, aware that they would no longer see Jesus in person, but eagerly awaiting God's gift of the Holy Spirit.

The Ascension.

On the next festival day, Peter was praying with the disciples when suddenly the whole room was full of a rushing, mighty wind, and it seemed as if flames of fire were present upon every person. But each one knew that God was with him – and each was filled with God's Spirit.

Peter led the disciples outside, and they began to speak to the crowds. The people were amazed. "We all come from many different lands," they said, "but we can each hear in our own language."

Then Peter told them that God had sent His Holy Spirit to dwell within them, as He had promised, and this could happen now because Jesus, whom they had crucified, had been raised up by God to be their Lord.

Some Jews did not understand this, but three thousand asked to be baptised, showing that they were true believers in Jesus.

Pentecost – preaching to the crowds.

One afternoon Peter and John went to the Temple to pray. There was a beggar sitting at the gate who had been lame all his life. He asked Peter and John to give him something.

"I have no money," said Peter, "but what I have I will give you. In the name of Jesus Christ – walk!"

He helped the beggar to stand up. The man felt strength in his ankles and began to walk. He went into the Temple to give thanks to God. Afterwards he began to leap about, so excited was he at the thrill of walking. The people came running to see, for they recognised the man, now jumping for joy, as the crippled beggar.

Peter spoke to the crowd. "It is faith in Jesus which has cured this man," he said.

Many became believers; but Peter and John were arrested by the Temple guards.

The lame beggar is healed.

Peter and John were brought before the Council of the High Priest. They were forbidden to teach another word about Jesus.

But Peter replied, "Is it right for us to listen to what you say, rather than what God says? For we cannot help telling others what we have seen with our own eyes." After a warning, they were released.

Still they continued to preach, for they knew that God wanted them to proclaim His message despite opposition. And opposition there was. On a number of occasions they were arrested, imprisoned and beaten.

Some time later King Herod ordered that James, brother of John, should be put to death. When he saw that this pleased the Jews, he imprisoned Peter. But the believers prayed earnestly to God to save Peter. One night while Peter was asleep with soldiers on guard at the door, an angel appeared in the cell.

Peter in prison.

"Get up quickly," the angel said to Peter.

Peter's chains fell off, and when the angel told him to put on his sandals and cloak, he did so automatically, as if in a dream.

"Follow me," said the angel, and led Peter right past the guards and out of prison. Then they reached the big iron gate leading out to the city. It opened for them and the angel vanished. Peter was free! He realised then that God had sent the angel to rescue him.

He went to the house where the Christians met, and knocked on the door.

"Who is there?" called the girl who came to answer.

"It is Peter," he replied. She was so surprised that she ran in to the others without opening the door, saying Peter was there. "You are crazy!" they said.

But soon they realised that she was right. They welcomed Peter with great joy.

Peter's miraculous release from prison.

Gradually the group of believers in Jerusalem grew in number. The confident faith and assurance of the disciples helped others to believe that Jesus really was the Son of God, and that trusting Him gave them a new and better kind of life. Peter was one of the leaders of these believers, the founders of our Christian faith.

But Peter felt that he must take the Gospel message to other lands, too. He travelled more, preaching to the Jews wherever he found them.

Eventually he went to Rome, and there he suffered persecution and death, as his Master had done. On the orders of the Emperor Nero, very many Christians were put to death in Rome, and Peter was amongst them.

Some writers say that Peter asked to be crucified head down, as he was not worthy to die in the same way as his Master. Peter had been Jesus' faithful friend and disciple, a steadfast, rocklike apostle to his life's end.

Peter before Nero in Rome.

Series 522